"Daddy will always love and protect you"

by: Larry Hagner

Illustrations by:
Oliver Kryzz Bundoc

Boys, this book is dedicated to you.

Ethan, Mason, Lawson, and Colton,
being your dad has been the best part of my life.

At times, I have struggled with how to show you
how much I truly love you and how much each of you mean to me.

There were amazing days and epic memories.
There were also times when it was challenging along the way,
but overcoming them was where our good days and epic memories shined.

I want you to know that I love you guys no matter what
and my love for all of you will never change.
You guys are my rock, my foundation, and the best part of my life.

Love you,

Dad

I will never forget the first time I met you
and the first time I held you.

I knew my life would never be the same.

I whispered
"I will always love you.
I will always protect you.
I am your Daddy and
I will always be here for you
for the rest of my life."

As you got older, my love for you
only grew more and more.

No matter what you did,
it never changed how much I loved you.

"I will always love you.
I will always protect you.
I am your Daddy and
I will always be here for you
for the rest of my life."

Even when Daddy is at work
or away from you,
I am always thinking of you.

There isn't a moment that goes by
when I am not thinking about
how much I love you.

"I will always love you.
I will always protect you.
I am your Daddy and
I will always be here for you
for the rest of my life."

No matter where I am
or what I am doing,
I am always thinking about you.

You make me so happy
even when we are apart.

"I will always love you.
I will always protect you.
I am your Daddy and
I will always be here for you
for the rest of my life."

Even when daddy gets upset
because of a hard day.
I always love you.

"I will always love you.
I will always protect you.
I am your Daddy and
I will always be here for you
for the rest of my life."

Even when you make mistakes
and you are learning.

"I will always love you.
I will always protect you.
I am your Daddy and
I will always be here for you
for the rest of my life."

Even when you are scared
and need someone to hold you,
Daddy will always be here for you.

"I will always love you.
I will always protect you.
I am your Daddy and
I will always be here for you
for the rest of my life."

Even on days when you feel sad and blue,
Daddy will be there to love you and hold you.

"I will always love you.
I will always protect you.
I am your Daddy and
I will always be here for you
for the rest of my life."

Even though we have other kids in our family,
Daddy will always love you!

You will always be special to Daddy.

"I will always love you.
I will always protect you.
I am your Daddy and
I will always be here for you
for the rest of my life."

No matter what happens in our life,
no matter where we are,
I will always love you
because you are so important to me.

"I will always love you.
I will always protect you.
I am your Daddy and
I will always be here for you
for the rest of my life."

63312581R00015

Made in the USA
Lexington, KY
04 May 2017